Rhiannon Owens

Rhianno

&

Asley

Ashley O'Keefe

Independently published

ISBN: 9798652581992

Contents

Foreword

Rhiannon and Ashley are passionate about writing. They both joined the (online) Merthyr Tydfil Creative Writing Group in 2019.

This collaboration came about due to a mutual appreciation of each other's work, which has developed into a friendship.

Though their writing styles are very different in many respects they share some common ground in the stories they tell, and the pictures they want to paint. They thought their poems would work well together so decided on this joint (ad)venture.

They are both incredibly grateful to the Merthyr Tydfil Creative Writing Group and those amazing members who've always supported them and kept their creative juices flowing.

Rhiannon and Ashley have never met in person and continue to communicate via their poems, messenger, and email, which is how they brought this project together.

It's time to meet Rhianno & Asley...

Rhianno

Under an infinite sky
Beneath the setting sun,
A mountain in the distance
The place it had begun,

A mould now sadly broken
A species almost extinct,
Nose-horned, odd-toed
But still so distinct,

Rhianno's thick dermal armour
Standing proud and strong,
Scary on the outside
Inside, seeking to belong,

Beneath the hard exterior
Amongst her silent tears,
A heart of gold, telling stories of old
Tales of her hopes and fears.

Ashley O'Keefe

Asley

'ASLEY stalks the earth
Lays waste to all in his path
With flames of hatred...'

I am Asley
spat from the loins of the earth.
Hellborn beast,
Master of destruction
on chaos, I feast.

The scorching heat emanates from him
the bright flowers and verdant grasses wither,
the mighty oaks bend and shake
roots torn from the ground
as it steams, and cracks and crumbles
from its very bowels an earthquake.
The water seethes and churns
boiling with rage
from the once placid
the once still lake.
Creatures in their hives
their sets, nests or burrows
all are incinerated
or slowly choked as they bake.

Asley strides across the land,
his terrible eyes opaque
with a thirst to destroy
that can never be slaked,
searching for mortals
to capture and rape,
he has lives to steal
souls he must take.
His touch is more deadly

more venomous than a snake
and everywhere there are charred remains
and bodies, craters
left in his fearsome wake.

"I am Asley
I rule all,
in my inferno
mankind falls.
None can escape me
I am Asley!"
the monster roars
and all is lost
to his furious force,
bones crunched
ground to powder,
consumed
by insatiable, fiery jaws.

Rhiannon Owens

NATURE / NATURAL WORLD:

The dawning sunrise
animals and plants gasping
man destroys all joy

Terrible Tranquillity

One rhino keeps watch,
solidly standing, tough leathery hide
keeping vigil in his thick armour
as a second rhino drinks at his side,
but the second rhino is still
his thirst not yet begun to be slaked
he stares into the eyes of his reflection
mournful eyes
not one mouthful of water he takes.

Time seems to have stopped
something has given him pause
the pink-hued water too placid
with no discernible source.
A stillness somehow unearthly
beneath a luminous deep pink sun
a tranquillity to the violet sky
belying the changes to come.

The change has been gradual
no cataclysmic interior rift
almost leisurely,
deceptively so
but still never too swift.
No big bang style impact
nor orchestra booming,
just little hints
of the earth's continuous drift.

Under these mighty grey beasts
something is constantly bubbling,
soil, rock and sand are sifting.

Beneath the calm, deceptive, pink beauty

the tectonic plates are always shifting
and rumbling.

Is the setting sun a little closer
than it's ever been to earth before?
Are the quiet waters just a prelude
to the final opening of a door?

The rhino still gazes down
unable to put his feeling into thought
a feeling of unease and restlessness
like earth's inhabitants are about to be caught.
Is the evening a little hotter?
A heat more oppressive, more intense?
Are the evening shadows a little deeper?
The dusty air, a little more dense?

Why does a shiver run across his spine?
Why do his muscles tense?

A change is on its way
a new world is dawning
this vibrant, fierce beauty of nature
is a sign, an omen, a warning.

How to make them understand
the momentousness of the event
the dinosaurs never saw it coming
their savage ending, a new epoch
that must have been heaven-sent.
Did the terrible lizards also stand
under a foreboding, effervescent orb,
sensing but not understanding
something far too final for them to absorb?

The second rhino stands frozen too

two creatures beneath the magenta glow.
Innocent, not realising that all is lost
caught in this beautiful, terrible,
final tableau.

Rhiannon Owens

A Dying Sun

The quiet, the peace, the tranquillity
Nature and Rhino as one,
The blood-red glow on the water
Reflects from a dying sun,

The end of a day at a waterhole
The end of a way of life,
Every day it's coming closer
The Hunter brings a knife.

Ashley O'Keefe

Infinite Dream

A curtain of white water
Cascading down,
An infinite dream
Like an elegant gown,

A place of stillness
With a deafening roar,
A force of nature,
A place to explore,

Beautiful, yet brutal
A spectacular chill,
Power and brilliance
A tranquil thrill.

Ashley O'Keefe

Sights Unseen

Beautiful untamed woodlands
Weeping willows form tunnels of green,
Gently curving along forgotten riverbanks
Dappled by sunlight, hiding sights unseen,

A clear river of floating lily pads
Nesting ducks in the shade of tall reeds,
The river is soft and wending its way
Over pebbles of ancient deeds.

Ashley O'Keefe

Psithurism

Psithurism, a new word for me
the rustling of the leaves dancing in a tree
a sound that carries on the breeze
as its branches are gently stroked and teased.

The trees are talking without words
they whisper the secrets of the universe
they murmur in undertones to one another
the elder to the oak
as they hum and sigh like lovers.

Stirring and swishing is their communication
the softest of sounds swirl, a susurration
that soothes and calms
falls pleasantly on our ears
the musicality of nature, a song for the present and future
a song from yester-year.

All this imagery from a simple little word
all the thoughts conjured up
from a subtle sound heard,
Psithurism calls to us
with sensuous voice
and we are seduced, stop to listen
in the Psithurism we rejoice.

Rhiannon Owens

Flower of the Sky

The iridescent glow of the butterfly
Serenity on petal-wings,
The flower of the sky
A swirl of dancing colours she brings,

Her delicate beauty in the summer sun
As sweet as the nectar she seeks,
Raising her wings, fluttering by
From cocoon to flight with mystique.

Ashley O'Keefe

Majesty

Noble creature of the skies
Flying on a lofty breeze,
Spreading wings; colossal
Gliding through clouds with ease,

Powerfully dominating the sky
Talons carrying twisted prey,
Beating the sultry air
Its plunder on a tray,

Soaring high above
Watching the world below,
A vast bucolic blanket
Hunting, swooping low.

Ashley O'Keefe

Auras of Sunlight

The sun is parting the drifting clouds
and sketching a golden halo around the trees,
smiling on the bold flirtatious blooms,
with kisses for shyly peeking shoots
to gently set them at ease.

Go to the window and look at the flowers
feel the breeze on your cheek,
and hear the birds sing.

Feel the sunshine kissing your skin
take a deep breath, draw it in
that sweetness in the fresh air,
the sweetness that is Spring.

As the days venture further into Summer
they grow brighter, they stretch longer
and the sun is a fiery orb in the sky
her hot, penetrating rays are stronger.

Lie on your back in the verdant grasses
time seems to stop
though you've been here for hours,
dreaming pure and honeyed dreams
lazily trailing fingers through
soft leaves and silken flowers.

The trees cast light and shadow
on your face
dappled patterns of sun and shade,
you're so still in your grassy bower
and you stay until the sunlight fades...

but tomorrow you'll be back

with dew saturating your behind,
pollen tickling your nose
sunshine warming bare arms and legs
breeze blowing away cobwebs,

and birdsong soothing your mind.

Rhiannon Owens

Crow

A silhouette against the autumn sky cut from the canopy of dawn.
The once bare branches of a great tree weighted down with black
shadows.

SUDDENLY… the blackness moves.
The SILENCE is broken by raucous crows… CAWING… fidgeting
… FLAPPING their tarry wings.

They watch with emotionless EYES…

A single crow descends from the autumnal air to the blood-soaked
ground littered with carcasses. With its ebony beak, it PECKS and
PULLS at the entrails of the fallen.
Soon the battlefield is a mass of crows; SQUABBLING, beating
their wings, crying out through a sea of darkness.

Ashley O'Keefe

Windmilling

Kaleidoscopic
in sunlight it pirouettes
to a coastal breeze

Iridescent Sky

A beautiful optical phenomenon
this scattering of sunlight
such irisation in the sky
a rare and heart-lifting sight.

Swirling pastel colours
lit up by the sun
vivid in the soap bubble cloud
a display of Nature just begun.

It could be small water droplets
that have led to this unusual scene
or perhaps it is tiny ice crystals
which created a mother-of-pearl sheen.

Whatever it is that gave to us
this breathtaking iridescence
I'll be smiling still and thinking of it
long after the rainbow cloud's evanescence.

Rhiannon Owens

Rainbow

A mist... moisture-laden air...
A rainbow arching across a lighten sky,
A painting with no canvas bringing joy without words,
A firework of bold colours on our dreariest of days,
A spectrum of light rays to uplift the soul,
A natural phenomenon... a daydream...

Ashley O'Keefe

Here Comes the Rain Again

The clouds are swollen
not a lot, not yet fit to burst
but heavy with ripening promise.

They've promised us
that the rain is coming soon;
Tonight!

The rain doesn't threaten,
the clouds are white
but the centres are grey-tinged,
with a rich, sumptuous filling
and they are gathering, gathering...

Rain the sweetest promise on the horizon,
no clammy, tempestuous threat.

The flowers smile up from the hard-packed, thirsty earth,
that is cracking with melancholy despair.
The cat exposes her belly longing for her fancy, fur coat to be
cooled,
while her green, plastic bowl sits empty
its round, shiny mouth sucking greedily,
fruitlessly, at dry, arid air.

I open my mouth to catch the plump, delicious drops.
Waiting, waiting…

We love the beautiful sunshine
that bathes us all in a loving, hopeful light,
but please Rain,
rain down on me!

Let us dance beneath your invigorating, irresistible needles of
rapture.
Just a little sweet relief,
not for too long.

We crave your hard, slanting kisses
but are fickle creatures,
tiring of you quickly.

Rhiannon Owens

Spirits Soaring

Hat blown off… brolly inside out
Fresh air was needed without a doubt,
A gust of wind and wild sea spray
The pounding waves roar across the bay,

The wind now lashing, hair wildly whipped
With backward steps, lean forward ripped,
Crashing waves, boats in mooring
This gusty wind sends spirits soaring.

Ashley O'Keefe

Splash of Colour

A little splash of colour
On a grey wet day,
Upon the canopy above
The rhythm of the rain,

Water gently bouncing
Each drop a clear beat,
Waterfalls cascading,
Splashing around your feet,

Like dancing through a movie
Or romantic city street,
A sea of rainbow colours,
Springing off the music sheet.

Ashley O'Keefe

WINTER:

cold winter sunlight
last blooms tremble - hope abounds
frozen knickers sway

Chilled to the Bone

Cold nose and ears
Hair whipping in serpentine coils
Icy blasts of wind
Leave me breathless
Leeches all my body heat away
Eddying crisp packets attack
Drenched down to my knickers.

The cold and rain bite at me
Orgasmic cacophony up above.

Torrential tears from Heaven
Hedonistic tango of the elements
Eyes red and raw from this barrage.

Battling through these forces
On leaden, sodden legs
Not daring to let go of my bobble hat
Extra layers are no defence.

Rhiannon Owens

Icy Hand

The evening winter wind slaps its icy hand across the face of the
homeless,
The cold and hunger gnaw at their bones,
Sitting, cradling knees in doorways, weakness creeps ever closer,
Tiredness looms, quietly shutting down as the night wears on and
temperatures plummet...
The morning winter wind slaps its icy hand across the face of the
homeless,
With dead eyes, they turn the other cheek...
They feel the icy hand no more...

Ashley O'Keefe

Winter's Embers

The crackle of ice underfoot
The bite of winter's teeth,
The crystal joy
The brilliant rays
The snowflakes on the heath,
The woollen hat
The steamy breath
The poetry in my soul,
The call of winter's embers
The spring for flowers to grow.

Ashley O'Keefe

Winter Solstice

On this day the Norsemen would kindle dry sticks,
coax them into bright, dancing flame
and spend the night drinking good, sweet ale,
recounting tales of the 'houl' the wheel of the Sun
while pagans tell of 'Yule' emerging from Samhain.

For now is the time when the Druids gather
to celebrate the Goddess giving birth to the Sun,
a cycle of rebirth and regeneration
ensuring that the turning of the wheel is never done!

Locked in a fertile embrace young lovers will sigh and groan,
She the Holly, the rich red Lifeblood,
He Mistletoe, white life-giving seed.
New life from the Heart of Winter, a celebration of all that is good.

For the sun does not forlese the darkness,
nothing is ever entirely lost, only altered or reborn
in this constantly turning wheel of life
the world is evergreen, something to celebrate
not to mourn.

Rhiannon Owens

Frozen Glass

The world is silent, muffled
despite the children skating on the frozen lake.
The ice has many shades, hues,
different depths, prisms of light
on an impenetrable surface.
Sometimes translucent, always multi-faceted,
sometimes frosted with intricately patterned soft snowflakes.
Mirror reflections, winter sunlight bouncing off smooth,
unyielding glass.

The *sshhttt sshhttt sshhttt*
of cruel blades scraping, skimming over ice.
Not always clear
there are shifting shadows too, in this icy lookout.
Nothing uniform in this maze of mirrors,
this crystallised cavern.

I press my hands,
my cold white hands
against the ice,
seeking light, life, warmth.
I push and push,
hammer with urgent yet hopeless fists
while my freezing heart ices over,
all over again.
Cold hands
colder heart.

Sshhttt sshhttt sshhttt;
those blades so near, they flash tantalisingly close
but could be light-years away.

A little boy approaches, wobbling on his skates,
tumbles, slides across the ice

and just for one fleeting moment
he sees me,
almost nose to nose
a moment suspended in time
'Help me'...
He scrambles to his feet, skates clumsily but speedily back to his
friends
already forgetting what he thought he saw.
He is frightened.
I am petrified.

My nails are broken,
bloody and torn from scratching scratching
scratching at this prison of ice.
My mouth is open
stretched wide in a silent scream,
a desperate, soundless plea to be back with the living.

Above me are more children,
all pink-cheeked, red-nosed
bundled up cosy,
toasty in knitted scarves, bulky mittens and oversized earmuffs.

They do not see my hands reaching up to them,
beseeching them.
They do not see
my face pressed hard against the ice
sobbing tears of frozen glass.

Rhiannon Owens
(Thanks to Ashley for suggesting 'Frozen Glass' as the title!)

Winter

Winter... the dawn of spring, its beauty takes me by the hand. An ice-covered lake awaits the sun through trees in denuded form. Through the charcoal silhouette of winter's naked rasp, comes the glitter of nascent RAYS to warm the SHIVER of the bitter wind. Soft flakes FLURRY and FALL as the cold, silent air weighs down on the FROZEN ground, and Old Man Winter extends his GNARLED and TWISTED hand.

Ashley O'Keefe

SPACE:

Silent Expanse

*Beyond marble earth
a boundless silent expanse
amongst silver stars*

A Celestial Event

Streams of cosmic debris
form a meteor shower
travelling at high speed
bursting into flower.
From one perceived fixed point
in the dark night sky
it's hard to imagine
such beauty way up high.
Smaller than a grain of sand
are most meteors that fall
disintegrating as they travel
destined never to meet Earth at all.
Sometimes there's an unusually intense
meteoric outburst or storm
at least 1,000 meteors an hour
far above and beyond the norm.
Perseids are the most visible
a breathtaking display
but a storming Leonid
will take your breath away.
These night sky illuminations
the meteors that radiate
and the comets and the stars
we desperately try to emulate,
with fairy lights and fireworks
to have a display that is terrestrial
but we can never have the splendour
of an event both phenomenal and celestial.

Rhiannon Owens

Asteroid

An expanse of rock and ice
Moving in deep space,
Heading for our planet
At a speed beyond all trace,

In its wake, a path of debris
A lonely fragment in the race,
But when it hits full force
It'll send oceans into space,

There's no hope for our future
This is our destiny,
A chunk of rock from outer space
Mother Earth obliterated; a catastrophe.

Ashley O'Keefe

Sea of Darkness

Adrift in a sea of darkness
Scattered diamonds all around,
Subtle light adorned
From sequins without a sound,

An ominous brittle silence
No gravity in this cold place,
Briskly floating by
Amidst a glistening sea of space,

Far off in the distance
A hurtling sound somewhere behind,
Suddenly shooting, shuttling past
At a speed that blows the mind,

Shaking... Rattling... Rolling...
Plummeting through space and time,
Within a metal capsule
In fear and awe of the sublime,

Entering the earth's atmosphere
A blazing fire, alight,
Gravity forces pulling, dragging
Like a fire of anthracite,

Within the space of minutes
Intense heat finally passed,
From out of the sky, an object
Previous travels, been surpassed,

Slowed by air resistance
Toward the earth in free fall,
Parachutes ejecting, floating
New discoveries for all,

Drifting on the ocean
Gazing up at wonderous skies,
Beyond, the vast empty loneliness
Galaxies erupt with a thousand eyes.

Ashley O'Keefe

25

Venus

The brightness of Venus
our sister planet
outshone only by our Moon,
in the Night Sky.

Our eyes are drawn to her fiery passions,
a shining Goddess way up high.

Venus looks so very beautiful
indeed, she's Goddess of Beauty and Love
but she's a temptress, the seducer of men,
though she glows so purely up above.

You must never mess with her
your fingers will be burned.
Volcanic Venus spewing out
clouds of sulfuric acid,
any unwanted advances will be spurned.

So lovely yet so volatile
choking you with reflective clouds opaque.
She lives for hedonism and sex,
but on her terms, and
she'll vaporise you
if you presume to take.

Rhiannon Owens

MOON:

*does her pale face dream
of golden sunshine instead
of eternal shade?*

Goddess of the Moon

The tawny owl's hooting
and werewolves are howling.
Cats are patient and vigilant,
as nocturnal creatures are prowling.

It's a full Moon tonight,
She lights up the sky,
with serenity and strength
yet somehow still wild,
wild like Artemis, Her Guardian,
and this Moon Her Child!

She will wax and She will wane,
a mirror image of life.
Phases of joy and of pain,
patient reflection in times of strife.

... and some of us lie weeping
our stuffing knocked out
by life's many cruelties,
wondering what it's all about?

...but the Moon is a constant
a bittersweet sight,
reminding us all
that day follows the night.
She's timeless and breathtaking
makes my heart hope,
that those of us suffering
will find means to cope.

Goodnight brave Artemis,
sweet, chaste and free.

Send one of your arrows
of endurance to me!

Rhiannon Owens

Mother Moon

Radiant in the light of her sister the sun
More beautiful than even the stars,
Mother Moon sings softly, sweet lullabies
To her children, Jupiter and Mars,

Gracing the blackness with her brilliance
Beaming brightly across clear skies,
She reflects all the beauty, the streaming light
Of the daytime star in her eyes,

In her warm milky luminosity
Amid the Starlight of her glow,
A song in the eyes of the singer
Watching the earth's beating heart below.

Ashley O'Keefe

The Hunter's Moon of Snow

The radiant Snow Moon of February
larger than life, a 'Storm Moon'
such luminosity in the light of it
light of this moon, au Clair de la Lune.

The 'Hunger Moon' it was known
to the American tribes of the North,
in the hard hunting conditions of mid-winter
with food scarce and hard to source.

They would stare up at this Moon
in the desolate, unforgiving terrain
but still give thanks, respecting Nature
despite frozen ground, and vast craggy plains.

Heads bowed this circle of elders
in spiritual ritual, each tribe's varied traditions
hope offered for sighting of buffalo
as the Snow Moon watches over all,
and she listens.

All over the World, she has watched
and listened to many a prayer,
but for these noble, dauntless tribes
she feels a fierce, protective flare.

Snow Moon of mid-winter
luminous in the night sky
glowing Clair de Lune
'Hunter's Moon' way up high.

Rhiannon Owens

Hina

Haunting lullabies echo
Across distance and time,
Riding the wind
Amongst the stars, her shrine,

In my dreams, she whispers… calling out to me,
Vividly shining over… the silent silver sea,

Her eyes piercing brightly
Into the starry night,
As she opens them wide
We dance beneath her light,

In my dreams, she whispers… calling out to me,
Vividly shining over… the silent silver sea,

Hina the Moon Goddess
Mistress of the flood,
Mahina's many faces
Singing softly to her beloved,

As the waxing moon; creatrix
A warrior spirit at the full moon,
As the waning moon; old and wise
Overseeing death in her dark moon.

Ashley O'Keefe

WOLF:

In her eyes serene
with fur coat glossy and thick
she stares at the moon

Howling at the Moon

I'm dancing in the dark
I'm howling at the moon
I dance with the wolves
to my own beat, my own tune.

I'm a poor man's Wolverine, a wild changeling
I'm the spirit of Lady Macbeth, see me dance, hear me sing.
Under the January night sky, in my torn and bloodied shirt
howling at this Wolf Moon
in the shadows of the trees, I hide, I pounce, I lurk.
I can't run with the Pack, I am not one of them
they do not trust my scent, they sense the blood and fear of men.

I can feel the madness growing, I'm tearing at my hair
I'm gazing at my palms, but no hair is growing there.
Spots of blood I can see
in the moonlight a fluorescence
but I washed them so many times!
Is this the blood the wolves can sense?
Crazed, the blood smeared around my mouth
mingles with the froth and foam
I'm laughing, snarling, ranting,
I know I can't ever go back home.

I'm dancing in the dark
I'm howling at the moon
I dance all alone
dancing to a lonely tune.

The Moon looms full, they say a man lives there
but they say it's made of cheese, the man in his hard cheese lair.
I throw my head back and laugh, laugh until I cry,
because the moon is made of cheese, and I must surely die.
I shake my fists at the man in the moon

I beg at him, imploring
the blood pulses between my ears
my temples pound, I'm roaring.

The devil's on my shoulder, and there's a demon in my brain
I've taken lives tonight, I've caused unbearable suffering and pain.

You see this blood on my hands, all this blood, it isn't mine
see the blood that isn't there, that in the moonlight doesn't shine?

I can feel my fangs growing, can feel them with my tongue
tiny, sharp budding canine teeth - that can tear through heart,
through throat, through lung.

This monster growing inside me; a deadly, ancient curse
but at night I can rip off my mask, in the daylight, it is worse
as my madness grows and grows, matched only by my bloodlust
any of my former life has now been ground into dust.
Every day has been more of a struggle, to keep it in place that
mask
it's so hard to keep control, not let it slip, it's become a Herculean
task.

I'm dancing in the dark
I'm howling at the Moon
I'm crying and I cannot stop
because they're coming for me soon.

I know this because I looked at my reflection
in a lake, though I didn't want to see
the cold, hard reality that proved
that the only monster here is me.

Rhiannon Owens

Wolf Moon

Skimming earth's shadow
As saliva DRIPS,
Is the sepia moon
Of a penumbral eclipse,

On the crest of the hill
A silhouette; BLACK,
A HOWLING wolf sings
And the pack ECHOES back.

Ashley O'Keefe

Out of the Shadows

Stillness… Silence…
The darkness of pre-dawn, devoid of birdsong.
A musky scent, a rancid breath, saliva DROOLS from lips.

Out of the shadows… a low rumbling GROWL
Stalking… nostrils FLARE, gums curl.
Suddenly, GNASHING teeth, a throat RIPPED out,
In a FRENZY of feeding, SCREAMS cry out…

Stillness… Silence…

Ashley O'Keefe

Lone Wolf

The Huskies have been spooked by something.
I shield my eyes but it's hard to see anything at all
in this blizzard with the fat flakes of fast-swirling snow.
I jump down from my makeshift sled,
grumbling a little,
clap my animal skin gloves together to free them from the crust of
ice,
and pull my fur-lined hat down tighter.

A shape by a tree, blurred in the relentless flurry
but as I get closer I can see it's a girl,
well, a woman;
a breathtakingly beautiful woman.
Trembling all over, her leg bleeding, caught in an animal trap.
'It's okay, it's okay' I reassure her as she jerks away from me,
almost snarling in her fear and distrust.
I fetch some tools from the sled and I soon have her free.
She's disoriented, white teeth chattering from cold and fright.
'You must come home with me' I coax her with my words, and
though she still seems fearful
she dips her head in acquiescence.

We sweep and glide through the sparkling snow
and she gasps and laughs in exhilaration
her laughter like beautiful pearls of ice
pinging musically about the dense, snowy landscape.
I can feel her heart beating as she presses against me,
and I am throbbing
as she grips me tighter and growls out 'Faster! Oh faster please!'
and tips her head back, eyes closed
as we career down the winding track
sending up a fine, icy spray in our wake.

Back in my little hut by light of a kerosene lamp

I see that she is even more beautiful than I'd first registered;
eyes the bluest of blue,
eyes to drown in
and be happy to do it!
and the darkest wing of silken hair
swinging against her smooth cheek,
streaked with ethereal silver-white.
A wild, feral beauty;
Vulpine features.

She watches warily as I clean her wound and dab cool ointment
over it.
Proudly aloof,
her lips curl back from her teeth whenever it stings,
and she rears away from me slightly.
She watches me too, as I lay out thick, warm pelts and soft furs for
her to sleep in,
and as I undress
places her hands against
my unruly, furred chest,
the hair bristles beneath the jolt of her touch,
as do I.
We are both hot-blooded creatures.

'Marry me!' I blurt out impulsively.
Her eyes search mine, and I squirm inwardly under her level
penetrating gaze,
she cocks her head to one side
'You would want me this way - why?'
Then her gaze slips.
'Because I love you.'
'You could love me?' her eyes widen in wonder, and she says 'Yes,
we will marry.'

Yet, it wasn't to be…
I woke and she was gone

though the lingering heat of a soft kiss on my sleeping lips
is surely more than a dream.

I race outside and I can see footprints
though already the falling snow tries to erase them from the world,
I must follow her regardless of this blizzard.
I am tracking her,
heart lifting at every indentation of firm footstep
before me
but after an hour or more
they are gone, I've lost the trail
there are only animal tracks now
that lead up, up a steep incline.
I cannot go any further
I sink to my knees, as tears spill from my eyes,
but freeze on my cheeks.

I look up and see a majestic She-Wolf
standing way above me.
Savage, alluring beauty
darkly blue-grey coat, with sweeps of the purest white, and tips of
shimmering silver…
not Vulpine
Lupine!

but it's that level gaze,
with eyes of cobalt blue, that undoes me.
A tear glistening on a furry cheek
as the beast turns from me
to forge her own, solitary path…
and I turn too, desolate
with my own, lonely path to be forged.

Rhiannon Owens

Tooth and Claw

Lean and hungry
Lies in wait,
Pitiless eyes
White fangs; salivate

On misty moor
A groping wretch,
A moon eclipsed
A feast to etch

Climbing high
Leaping down,
Growling, tearing
Ripping gown

Amongst the tombstones
Tooth and claw,
A silent grave
Bestrew bones and gore.

Ashley O'Keefe

SEA / SAILING:

Opaque waters roil
sapphic sirens seduce me
song and sea claim me

Silent Waters, Stormy Heart

Her heart is in turmoil
as she looks out across the calm waters before her.
So still, so deceptively placid,
but she knows it's a different story
with undercurrents and riptides
hidden within the depths,
while further out waves
clash and roil, furious
at the trespassers from dry land.

Her husband was a sailor
but expert as he was
still a landlubber really.
His little boat dashed to pieces
on the savage rocks.
His body dashed to pieces
in the smash of the waves.

Her heart smashed in bits…

She stares out over the vast expanse
of water stretching far and wide,
infinite and unending.
The eerie light of the moon
cuts a gleaming path across the silent waters.

Her heart storms
as she sees her husband there in the distance
he waves and beckons.
Her heart bursts
and she walks into the cold,
unafraid as the moon lights her way.
The shimmering water hugs her shape
and her husband guides her

back to where she belongs…

With him.

Always with him.

Rhiannon Owens

Back to the Sea

Flashes of white tossed in the grey
Tumbling, they struggle against the gale,
Skimming the waves against the wind
Gracefully swaying, their supper rescind,

Beneath them the sea, a turbulent storm
Unforgiving, angry, unable to perform,
Tracing the curves of those briny hills
Inland they float to get food in their bills,

As the storm passes, they drift back to sea
The cries of the seagulls, they mock, and they flee,
Casting dark shadows, they squawk, they glide
They follow the moon; they drift with the tide.

Ashley O'Keefe

Uliet of the Oceans *(for Juliet)*

Swimmers, surfers, fishermen beware
for all of the sea is Uliet's lair,
she is Goddess and Monster
the Water Guardian.

Watching you as above her you float.
Watching you in your flimsy little boat.

Did you see her?
Did you catch a glint …
just there?
Her giant, all-seeing eye
in the sunlight's glare.
Seeing all,
seeing you
with her steady, azure stare.

Are the waves suddenly a little higher?
Is the boat rocking that bit more?
Are you wishing you were somewhere drier?
Not watching raucous seagulls dip and soar.

Are you suddenly all at sea
tossed about like so much flotsam?

Can you hear Uliet's rumbling
the thunderous roaring of her voice?
Isn't it time to get to dry land
while she is still giving you a choice!

Time to turn back, before you are harmed
leave Uliet and Her Oceans,
else succumb to a watery grave…
dragged down

down
down…

A captive in a whirlpool.
A captive in her arms.

Rhiannon Owens

Sailing

The sail stands proud
Salty breeze on my face,
With wind-whipped hair
The rope line I brace,

Gliding over water
Dancing through waves,
Piercing a path
Across oceans it paves,

In a seamless time
On a timeless sea,
The sun, the sea,
The birds and me,

Like a whispering lover
Calling out to me,
Sailing towards the horizon
Where I long to be.

Ashley O'Keefe

Beautiful View

Eyes like the Indian ocean
Pools of iridescent blue,
A sculptured face, cherry lips
All at sea with a beautiful view,

Hair cascades like waterfalls
Strands of molten bronze,
Crystal white teeth, perfectly carved
With body elegance of swans.

Ashley O'Keefe

MYTH / FOLKLORE:

The Watchman's Sorrow

There are one hundred
sad eyes on the Peacock's tail
born of jealousy

(Inspired by the Greek Myth of Argus The Watchman; the infidelity of Zeus
with Io, and Hera's jealousy).

Dwynwen and Maelon

By Dwynwen's father
their marriage forbade
he kept them apart
though pledges of love were exchanged.

Promised to another
the young maid was distraught
she asked God to make her
not love Maelon
comfort in prayer she sought.

Dwynwen was visited by an Angel
bearing a sweet potion
to make her forget him
and his lover's devotion,
and to turn him into a block of ice
but God gave her three wishes
she wished once,
twice, thrice.

She wished that Maelon would be thawed,
then she wished that the hearts of young lovers
might soar.
Her final wish was that she should never be wed,
she devoted the rest of her life to God instead.

The remains of her church can still be seen today
and her legacy lives on
when young lovers pray.
Their hopes and dreams of love always fulfilled
because of chaste Dwynwen
and her Maelon Daffodril.

Rhiannon Owens
(Saint Dwynwen, sometimes known as Dwyn or Donwen, is the Welsh patron saint of lovers. She is celebrated throughout Wales on 25th January).

Search for 'Life'

The roll of thunder
In a darkened Sky,
Conspiring Clouds
Scudding by,

High on the mountain
The swirling mist of time,
Four snorting horses
Their riders search for 'haim',

Rearing up, braying
Tarry muscle, untamed,
Reined hands, unpraying
Manes like flame,

Swooping down the mountains
Flying across the planes,
The horsemen of the apocalypse
And death is their name.

Ashley O'Keefe
('Haim' is of Hebrew origin meaning 'Life' and is pronounced 'Hime').

Firebird

Rising like a Phoenix
from the ashes, but alive with the flames,
burning so bright
like Margot Fonteyn
as she whirled
and took flight across the stage,
a vision in scarlet and titian.

She is garnet and rubies.

Enchanted,
we shield our eyes from The Firebird
but can't tear our vulnerable gaze away
as its powerful form
arcs across the endless skies,
a dazzling trail in its wake;
sunburst and fireworks.

Glowing embers
burst and crackle,
flaring into red-orange fire.

The eyes penetrate your soul
black as coals they blaze with a white-hot centre.
Fiery wings beat at and fan the ocherous flames,
which leap and curl…

and lap sensually in your mind
teasingly flickering,
licking suggestively
as you give in to dangerous passions.
Scorched; your fingers burned
with vermillion pain and need that flared
for a moment,

that sizzled
for a moment,
but was destined to be brief.

For this is a Bird of Paradise;
akin to an Old Testament Angel gripping a fiery sword,
orange and cardinal sin of desire.
A beauty that is both absolute
and terrifying in its ferociousness
as it burns through the Heavens,
and your heart.

A single glowing feather remains
sparking a path down to the ground.
It will always light your way,
should the darkness set in.

Rhiannon Owens
**(Inspired by the Russian fairytale of The Firebird, and also the beautiful
ballet that was born from it!)**

Sapphic Sea

More like the Sirens
of Odysseus's mythology
when they first drew her in.

She stood on the packed sand
warm between her bare toes,
while the sun glinted off the ocean
and the shattered shells around her.

Strangely erotic
the exciting depths of that sand,
hot to touch
but dig a little further
and so cool and fathomless.

The sun dipped low toward the waves
and I heard sweet song,
unbearably sweet
wrenching at my heart and soul.
Faraway figures beckoning,
willowy sylph-like silhouettes
alluring even from afar,
so irresistible.

I wanted, needed the touch
of these sapphic beauties.

Following their song
reckless, I walk into the water,
no fear from me
despite the waves growing ever higher.
The undertow pulls at me
but caresses my most sensitive bits,
and I cry out aloud
from the sheer pleasure of it.

They come to meet me
to take me,
all smooth limbed
and soft lipped,
fingers touching and stroking me
slipping inside
where I could never have imagined,
would never have dreamed
though I often yearned.

I roll on waves of ecstasy
press my head to their breasts.

Sinking below the surface
my bliss is interrupted,
eyes wide I finally see
the mermaid women for what they really are.

Sinewy, cold arms grip my
aching spent body.
Scaled fingers pinch,
green seaweed hair whips
shockingly against my blue skin.

Sea serpent Medusa.
Gorgon sisters;
they froze me with their song
and erotic promises.
Soulless eyes, devoid of any feeling
are the last thing I see,
the mollusc nails raking down my skin,
pulling at the pulsing,
sensual core of me
and I tremble and writhe.

I surrender.

Rhiannon Owens

Kites without strings

Kites without strings
Our rhythmic beat,
Freedom in flight
Our prey, they bleat,

Living in caves
Destined to decay,
Trapped in our slumber
'Tis the dragon's way,

At that moment they came
Ironclad Man,
Two-legged beasts
To annihilate our clan,

To end who we are
And all we could be,
In the dragon's glare
They're blind, they can't see,
Within the lair
Of our Serpent King,
In frenzy, cold-hearted
Blades cut, blades sing,

Stealing the prize
Taking our teeth,
For their decoration
And leaving no wreath.

Ashley O'Keefe

Succubus

In female form
She perambulates my dreams,
A seducer of men
I'm unable to scream,

A powerful seductress
Sexy and smart,
A night as her lover,
She won't steal my heart,

Tantalising and teasing
Egging me on,
Playing; toying
She jangles my Jong,

Her voluptuous curves
Flawless silk skin,
Caressing my body
My face, I just grin,

With skimpy leatherware
And long wavy hair,
She pleasures and pleases
Brings my attention to bear,

Straddling my body
She goes down for the kill,
Extracting my seed
Like a bird through its bill,

The passion is over
The pleasure is gone,
My Succubus lover
Is no longer the song,

No longer the goddess
A fiend and a fake,
Now a Night Hag before me
Under her paralysis, I quake.

Ashley O'Keefe

Incubus

My salacious incubus, my induced nightmare
injects his demon seed, penetrates with yellow stare.

He's taken me hard, made me low
sapping all of my strength,
using me with maleficence
thrusting with his cruel, hard length.

I scream out loud, struggle and shout
but he scoffs at exorcism
they can't cast him out,
they're moths to his flame, and
I'm trapped in an unholy prison.

Why do us mortals so easily succumb
to the Devil and his trickery?
To the bleak darkness that leaves us numb,
if it weren't for the flames we might see.

Bestial you tricked me,
but… did you really think me pure?
Anything you try to take from me,
I'll claw it back and more!

I clutched your bristly, sinewy torso
felt you bite deep into my breast,

I took your thick, barbed phallus
so I know I've passed the test.

Your seed I have nurtured
my light complementing your dark.
Now you are spent, the weak one,
and I?
I am the Devil Matriarch.

Rhiannon Owens

The Wild Hunt

'Tis the time of midwinter
The darkest part of the year,
Menacingly cold
Desolate silence to fear,

Alone in a bedroom
A young boy; awake,
He listens for the clatters
He waits for the shake,

Under the covers
Young eyes tremble; dart,
Anticipating the nightmare
About to impart,

The wind has died
The snow falls on the ground,
There's a deathly silence
A warning sound,

Out on the trackway
A fresh crunch in the snow,

56

A woman leaves footprints
To meet her new beau,

Suddenly in the distance
An announcing horn calls,
Pressing and dissonant
Falls from the great halls,

Her eyes open wide
She shivers with dread,
She knows it's the sound
Of the restless dead,

Sweeping through the forests
In a ferocious storm,
They come, the spectral riders
With their nocturnal swarm,

Stampeding steeds
Hounds from hell,
Barking, snarling
A howling swell,

Crows and Ravens
Birds of death,
Pecking innards
Taking breath,

Through forest hollows
In and out of the trees,
Like slithering serpents
at very high speeds,

Twisting, turning
Fauna run and hide,
From the meandering demonic
Terror 'Roller Coaster' Ride,

At the front of the horde
The Lord of the Dead,
Odin the Norse God
Rides Sleipnir the eight-legged,

A ghostly leader
With his hunters and hounds,
Flies through the cold night
With its howling wind sounds,

A riotous parade
The Phantom Army of the night,
Thundering along the trackway
Taking souls in their sight,

The young woman: hair whipped
Throws herself to the ground,
In the middle of the track
With snow all around,

She lies in the snow
She holds her breath,
Her soul in the balance
Between life and death,

A whirlwind runs over
Like a train on the track,
Sweeps her up for a moment
Then throws her straight back,

Within but a moment
Like the end of a song,
The demonic horde
Has come and gone,

She lay in the cold
In shock and in fear,

She lived through the hunt
But her eye shed a tear,

Some ethereal being
Has planted his seeds,
She felt it in passing
Her bitten lip bleeds,

Into the town
The Wild Hunt rides on,
Taking mortal souls
And singing death's song,

Winding through houses
Possessing new blood,
The horde rides the wind
Like a river in flood,

Back to the dwelling
The place of the dead,
The hall of the fallen
There's a boy's empty bed,

Possessed or devoured
Body and soul,
By the bloodthirsty horde
Who ravaged and stole,

A perilous, seductive,
Destructive thing,
Woe to the encountered
No more shall they sing.

Ashley O'Keefe
(Based on Scandinavian Folklore of the Norse Myth about 'The Wild Hunt'.)

ANGELS:

A celestial
light; benevolent being
wings rippling pure white

An Angel Sighs

He wanted to keep her with him
so she'd always be close by,
but didn't know
that when you clip an Angel's wings
they start to pine away,
they die…

white feathers spilling onto the ground
some carried away up high,
swirling on the fresh, cool breeze…

and so now he's losing her anyway
she's fading fast
watching her, he cries
as her blue blue eyes gaze up
at the blue of the blue blue sky.

He should have let this Angel soar,
he should have encouraged her to fly.

Rhiannon Owens

Empty Tree

I once saw an angel
Her feathers falling all around,
I picked them up and kept them
I glued them, made them bound,

I placed them in my garden
I hung them from my tree,
In a dream, words were spoken
I think I heard her plea,

In my dream, she was flying
At that moment soaring free,
The next day in my garden
I found an empty tree.

Ashley O'Keefe

Hallucination

A breeze that chills
Like icy fingers through hair,
Through the mist
At a vision, I stare,

In human form
Emitting light,
Glowing from within
Wings fleecy white,

In the gentle wind
Feathers ripple bright,
An angel of beauty
Within my sight,

A voice in my head
Has passed no lips,
Calming and soothing
Like Jackanory scripts,

Suddenly, a gust
Dust blows in my face,
I clear my eyes
To find an empty space...

Ashley O'Keefe

Behind the Old Door

There's an old door at the bottom of the garden
half-hidden by ivy and moss
peeling green paint renders it more hidden still.
Camouflaged in the canopy of weeping willows
an unremarkable door, surrounded by wild rambling roses
but the thought of what might be behind gives me a thrill.

It's like I'm in 'The Secret Garden'
my heart pitter-patters
fluttering in my weak, wasted chest.
I grasp the rusted, iron key
turn it in trepidation, push open the wooden door
though I've been told that I must rest.

A beautiful maiden stands before me
bedecked with a pretty, ribbon festooned bonnet
and with a sweet smile reaches out to me.
Her frock is quaint yet becoming
her radiant purity fills the air
with her, I am strong, robust, healthy.
I walk beside her and she sings to me
birds chirrup in a bright, blue sky
I pluck a flower and shyly offer it to her.
She smiles, twining it into her bonnet
picks up fallen apples, pops them in her wicker basket
but selects the juiciest, shiniest of the fruit for us to share.

Up in my sickbed, my pale body prone
I float in a morphine dream
with a peaceful smile on my face…
and as the last breath escapes me
the lovely maid gently grasps my hand
and I know I've come to a better place.

Rhiannon Owens

GHOSTS:

The stealer of breath
comes at night, mouth clamps to mine
I succumb to her

Shadows of Love

The young lovers are hand in hand,
she stands on tiptoe to kiss her beau
in the shifting shadows of the graveyard.
Made selfish in their desire
nothing else matters to them but this, now.
Deep passionate kisses
tongues thrusting
hands groping,
buttons and zips a momentary frustration.
Heat from their bodies permeates the air.
An owl regards them crossly,
he's hungry, and they have warned off his dinner.

The lovers sigh and moan,
the blank faces of the tombstones watch silently
as their limbs intertwine.

Deep groaning
a longing ...
but not the lovers…

The longing of the spirits who drift between the graves,
their bodies cold and rigid,
locked in wooden boxes
beneath the unforgiving earth,
only worms to embrace them now.
They sigh and shift
longing for warm kisses
yearning to be touched.
Tender caresses
clumsy fumbling
and frenzied sex.
Hot breath and heightened heartbeats
pupils dark with desire.

They long for this physical, life-affirming act of love
but have only ghosts of lovers,
ghosts of memories…
they watch hungrily, these pale spectres
who still dream...

and the lovers love on oblivious,
wrapped up in each other flesh seeking flesh.

Rhiannon Owens
**(Thanks to Ashley for suggesting 'Shadows of Love' as the
title ❤)**

Ignominious

A room… a chair…
I sit… I stare…
Through my monochrome musings
A chill in the air…

Wallpaper peels, dampness beneath
Crumbling walls… a picture of grief,

Under my veil, a cloud of grey mist
Darkness lingers… do I really exist,

Rotting floorboards, a broken frame
Old pieces of glass… a face with no name,

Clutching a fairy that fell from a tree
If I could go back there, I'd go down on one knee,

I wanted the present but needed the past
My eyes brim with tears, the die has been cast,

Suddenly, the air shimmers, it warps, and it twists
In a flash of light, amongst headstones, I've missed

Her name on the headstone, if only I could be…
Then her hand reaches out… my future is free…

Ashley O'Keefe

Ghosts of Grief and Shadows

The nursery is deathly still,
the cot is cold and bare
a woman sits clutching a stuffed toy bunny,
in an ancient wicker chair.
Sometimes she fancies she hears a footstep
creaking on the stair
but she stopped bothering to check long ago,
there was never anyone there.

She lost her husband and two children
an infant girl, a sturdy boy
snatched away by life's cruelty
her only comfort's this inanimate toy…
but there is someone there
though she is oblivious
drowning in a gallery of tears
a voice whispers and echoes:
'I'm here for you, I feel your loss too
please open your eyes and your ears…

Open your heart,
open your mind
I'm here for you, I miss them too.
I'm here, I'm here, let me in
let me mourn with you.'

A figure in a portrait
appears to be weeping
shifting, stretching, elongating
but the woman may as well be sleeping,
locked away in a sea of memories
locked in a private hell,
she is more ghost than the one who is
in her stunted grief she's a husk,

just a bereft and empty shell.
Wind howls around the ramparts
she squeezes her eyes shut tight
thinks she sees her husband
stepping into the light,
and surely that's the gurgle of a baby
the laughter of a strapping young lad
but there is only one spirit in this house
the one she refuses to see
the one being driven mad:

'Please see me, I'm just here
you need only turn around
look at me here, reaching out of the shadows
I'm here, so easily found.'

… but the woman turns her back on the darkness,
turns her back on a glimmer of hope
sets down the bunny, and with purpose
grasps a thick length of rope.
The ghost sighs, exhales
screams, sobs and moans:
'Don't do this, you mustn't.
I'm here you aren't alone!'

Grasping at the woman
seeing only too well her deadly intent,
knowing she has to get through to her
for this is why the ghost was sent.
The woman is trying to fashion a noose
but the rope keeps falling to the floor
it feels as though someone is snatching it away
'Stop it please!' she sobs, she implores.

She wants to see little fists beating air
voices calling her to reunite with them,

in a realm beyond this dreary world
a world not of mortal women or men.
Instead, she sees a wraith creeping
stealing the rope away
into those lengthening shadows,
but she does not WANT to stay.

'Go away, AWAY' the woman screams
'I don't want to be here anymore'
then a silhouette is in front of her
a shape, a voice she knew before.
At first, she dares not believe it
she claps her hands over her ears,
squeezes her eyes shut again
it might not be real, she fears.

A voice thick with tears speaks to her:

'I'm here, I'm back to share your pain
because I love you above all others,
you aren't alone, I'll stay with you
because I am your own dear Mother.'

The woman's tears fall freely
the ghost becomes substance
materialises,
come back to her to share her burden
out of love she now realises.
She gives a sob and a smile -
How had she not believed?
and she falls into her mother's arms,
no longer lonely
the two of them able to grieve.

Rhiannon Owens

Chill in the Air

Does my mind play tricks
Am I hearing things,
Is my head full of thoughts
In a dream that sings...

A look into the past
A story of old,
A night that is dark
A tale that is cold,

There's a chill in the air
A shimmering mist,
A whimpering child
Does she even exist,

A desolate soul
Mournful and lonely,
Clutching her ragdoll
This is her story...

Like an icy shower
Or the arctic air,
Every warm feeling
Sucked out by her stare,

Her soulless eyes
Reaching within,
Beseeching my soul
To search, to begin,

Now a game of charades
She hovers, she flows,
Passing through walls
She comes and she goes,

It's all such a mystery
It doesn't make sense,
From out of her darkness
The fear, the suspense,

Then up to the attic
Gently rocking, a chair,
A decaying body
With her featureless glare.

Ashley O'Keefe

I Still Stand

A Whisper...
Like the soft susurration of the wind in the trees,

A Shimmer...
Slowly into focus, clearer now, more sharply focused,

A Ghost...
An eerie moaning voice with heavy-lidded soulless eyes,
desolate, mournful, and lonely,

In its Gaze...
My mind robbed of emotion, frozen cold like a statue in a
graveyard, it beckons to me and I must, I want to stay here forever.
I open my mouth to speak, but no sound passes my lips,
My body crumples to the ground... Yet, I still stand.

Ashley O'Keefe

LOSS / SORROW:

Lonely in silence
feeling emptiness inside
I hold back my tears

Looking for Hedgehogs

The first night we were oblivious
but the next morning I saw the black droppings with the tapered ends,
and the evidence of a pathway of trampled grass.
We hoped it was the same one that came to visit the year before.
I didn't even mind that it cared not a fig for my flowers or shrubs.

Watching the telly, my husband having a last cigarette before bed,
but instead of heading straight upstairs
he bobs over to the window.
'What are you doing?' I say,
And he replies 'Looking for the Hedgehog.'

More evidence of your nocturnal visitations.
Further droppings, your passage to the cat food we provide
now suitably smooth and bare,
grass trodden into the boggy ground.

My husband opens the curtains and peers out
into the darkness.
'Looking for Hedgehogs?'
I say with a smile,
and he smiles
and fetches the torch, muting its glare with his capable hands.

A Hedgehog will tend to stick to
a tried and tested route,
and they are noisier than you might think.
Their droppings are their calling cards.

My husband keeps a faithful yet fruitless vigil,
but we leave food out every night.
'Looking for Hedgehogs' becomes our little joke

because he always is looking for our prickly guest with
undiminished optimism.

Sitting in the living room, pretending to read a book
I fancy I hear a noise outside the window,
and I look over to my husband
'Looking for Hedgehogs?' I say
to the empty room
a weak smile stretching chapped, bleeding lips

and no Hedgehog is foraging
trundling by,
on its nightly round.

I still look for Hedgehogs, but there is never any sign.

Rhiannon Owens
***(Inspired by my husband's nightly obsession with the Hedgehog that isn't
there! 🦔 🦔 🦔)***

Silence of Sorrow

Silence engulfs me, it captures my soul,
Caresses my skin, soothes my thoughts,
Hangs in the air; suspended in the moment,
Like dawn without birdsong: quiet, peaceful,
ominous, eerie,

The 'SOUND' of silence chills me to the bone,
It creeps, it whispers...
The screaming silence of sorrow.

Ashley O'Keefe

How Do You Like Them Apples?

My days as an Apple-knocker may be over
what with my cramped, arthritic hands
but my days of knocking back apples are not
I close my eyes and take a deep swallow of rough scrumpy
the loopy juice that defines me
as a sad, drunken sot.

My hands though sadly twisted
can just about manoeuvre the big plastic flagons
I carefully examine each for dregs, collect each and every
tittynope
into a pint glass
'Waste not, want not!' I would say to Frank
when he was here, and we'd raise a glass together
but now I'm alone on a slippery slope.

If I squint when I look at my reflection
I can pretend I'm still the rosy-cheeked maiden
one flutter of my eyelashes
making my Franky blush
but I'm not that naive
I'm wrinkled and my cheeks are sallow
eyes red and bloodshot from
quaffing and crying,
my 'rosiness' is just a warm, red alcohol flush.

My sweet, uncomplicated Franky
'Apple-knocker' my father would grunt
referring to his rural upbringing
but Frank and I were so in love
I didn't want the shallow sophistication of the city
I wanted to lie in the grass with Frank
go scrumping, and feel my heart singing.

I could get cross very easily

'*Come now Emily*' Frank would say
'*enough of this bobsy-die*'
and I'd huff and stamp my foot
my passions all a muddle
having a real hissy fit
but Frank would just keep smiling
until I couldn't help but laugh when he caught my eye.

Rolling in the hay
growing bolder with one another
and we were wed for 62 wonderful years
Frank's beautiful heart soon won over
my father and mother
… and now I'm alone
trying to find him in the murky orange depths
of the farmhouse scrumpy
lost in a thousand memories
as bittersweet and sharp as the scrumped apples
now fermented, decaying…

Oh, Frank! My husband, my heart, my lover!

Rhiannon Owens

Cusp

A song… irresistibly sweet… drifting on the wind,
Its words laced with sadness and grief, of sorrow and heavy heart,
A melody… purring to my soul, engulfing my being within,
An invisible cord pulling my final breath…
As I fall into permanent slumber, I smile.

Ashley O'Keefe

Shadows Remain

In the raw emotions of time
In the emptiness inside,
In the memories in my mind
In my life, I must find

In the darkness of my days
In my sorrow, there's no escape,
In a world, too hard to take
In a life without you is fake

In my heart, in my breath,
In the hollow of my chest,
In the shadows of the pain
In the ashes, shadows remain.

Ashley O'Keefe

Solitary Shame

The leaves of autumn blow and gather
They roll along the ground,
Rolling across the saddened grass
Resting against a headstone they have found,

There's a name engraved upon the stone
No face, just her name,
A man kneels helplessly in front of it
In his solitary shame,

His eyes brimming in drowning tears
An internal sobbing pain,
There's nothing left, no hope but fears
A life of choking rain.

Ashley O'Keefe

The Empty Chair

"A fire still burning
in me, that craves to consume.
Ash spills from my mouth."

The wooden chair before the cold, empty mouth of the grate is unoccupied - standing forlornly in the bare room with the dilapidated walls and peeling, faded paintwork. It hadn't always been this shabby. He remembers her, rosy-cheeked, stoking the cheerful flames of the fire. He can see her now in that plain, sturdy chair, the firelight glinting off her auburn curls, beneath the frilled cap.

No, he cannot bear to watch this, cannot relive this! He feels the grief and rage rise within him like the bitterest bile. His hands itch and curl into fists and he's before her once again, shaking her hard from side to side, throwing her to the ground - hearing the sickening crunch as her head smacks into the iron edge of the grate, and her body lolls there as floppy and lopsided as a ragdoll...and all he can think is that he must, must get rid of the body...and he must feed the orange and yellow maw of eagerly reaching, licking flames. The fire must never go out.

The fire burnt out long ago.

Rhiannon Owens

MENTAL HEALTH:

Behind the fake smile
lost in shadows of self-doubt
soul drowning in pain

We Don't All Wear Black

Am I happy?
Don't just assume,
even if my smile
lights up the room.

Am I confident
because I wear bright, bold colours
when I'm out and about?
Or is it my disguise
deflecting low self-esteem
and self-doubt?

I laugh and I love,
all is tranquil and calm
but there are ways that our brains
can internalise our self-harm.

I'm loud and I'm brash
so must have a thick skin.
Wrong again;
no one knows the contents
of this neatly packaged tin.

I don't have a job or kids,
so how can I be under pressure?...
Aren't there more layers to us?
Why do our lives need to be labelled,
our worth as people measured?
Next time you see someone
and for whatever reason
assume they're okay,
just remember that ...

we can all be vulnerable,
you can't always see
where the edges
are beginning to fray.

Rhiannon Owens

Broken

To put one foot in front of the other
To recall a happy thought or memory of a smile
To be worthy of love and joy...

Years of grief above my head
In a cloud that blocks the sun

TIREDNESS... like a veil over my skin; grey and cold,
DARKNESS surrounds the light,
Growing DARKER, the pain SHARPER,
SHADOWS follow the TEARS in my soul
Amongst the coldness; a void

In a sea of SELF-DOUBT, unable to swim
Creeping in SORROW, SINKING in the sand
The WEIGHT of it all PRESSING down on my shoulders...

Unseen... unheard... DARKNESS beyond measure,
This SILENT KILLER forever...

PAIN... too much to cope with,
too hard to deal with and so misunderstood...

Nobody cares. No one notices the horrible FAKE SMILE...
The BROKEN look in my EYES...

Ashley O'Keefe

Climbing Mount Everest

I toss and turn, sweating under the covers
my thoughts are racing, panicky
and I'm finding it difficult to breathe evenly.

My thoughts come thick and fast
but make no sense,
just half-formed words and sentences
that float in a choppy sea of worry.

Worry… Worry…

There's a pressure in my head, like a tight steel band crushing my skull.
How will I ever get a job?
Why can't I make friends?
Images of the hoarder's hell that my home has become
assault me.
My heart thumps and judders
at the thought of the mess I should be cleaning
but seems so wholly wholly
overwhelming.
Unobtainable.

Waiting for the phone to ring with the news of a loved one's death.
It's coming, I know it!
Daylight begins to creep into the room
I don't toss and turn any longer…
I freeze
I am frozen.
A useless lump under the stinking covers…
Who will I let down today?

Should I even get up?

What for? To slump miserably in front of the washing machine
defeated by a mundane, simple task that everyone manages
without even thinking about
without so much as batting an eyelid…
but to me seems mammoth, insurmountable
like climbing Mount Everest wearing slippers.

I don't have the energy to paste on that smile
the shit-eating grin of fakery,
because if I stretch my mouth too wide
I might shatter into a million pieces
cut to pieces on the shards and bleeding out
the facade tumbling, tumbling, tumbling…
Tumbling thoughts
jumbled thoughts
spiralling, dragging me down, down.

Should I even get up?
My limbs are too heavy to manoeuvre,
my brain is sluggish now.
Should I even get up?
I don't get up - I stare at the ceiling
as if the answers might be there
in the swirls of the ancient artexing.

Rhiannon Owens

A Lonely Road

Behind the smile, a soul in pain
With eyes a glaze, alone again,
A carousel, tension grows
In face, in limbs, in all my woes

Running, hiding
Needing purge,
Fight or flight,
A primal surge

Overthinking, overflow
A cup too empty, a cup too full,
My thoughts are racing, the volume's jammed
Brain on fire, my head's in sand

A mind replaying - future, past
Rapid breathing, heartbeat fast,
Stomach heaving, a storm within
Seeing, believing, I just can't win

Screaming body, screaming mind
There's just no logic, too weak to find,
Over the edge, overload
It's a long way back... a lonely road.

Ashley O'Keefe

*♥... a sweet sigh, a soft
kiss, Cupid's arrow did not
miss - this is our bliss... ♥*

An Ambient Passion

When we first met there was an undeniable spark
an electricity that fizzed and crackled
intensified by us living so far apart.
A whirlwind of passion
tumultuous, it carried us away
tossed on a storm, an inferno of feelings
you stole my heart that very first day.

Now we are married, the intensity has softened
our love is reflected in the silhouette of your smile
it echoes soundlessly in words we don't need spoken,
an ambience more gentle, and gestures understood
a twinkling in the eyes, an eyebrow pertly raised
but although we have moved on
from those first heady days
the echoes remain, and behind the serenity of love
an inferno still *rages*,
our blistering passion still *burns*
a white-hot passion that *blazes*.

Rhiannon Owens

Loved

As your loving eyes reach into my soul
Like sunlight through raindrops, where rainbows show,
In the sacred well, buried deep in my heart
My feelings, my emotions, spark passions in art,
Caught up in this divine spell of creativity
If not magic, I know not what else this could be,
Love is life's energy, love's who we are
I'm blessed and I'm loved, in abundance; by far.

Ashley O'Keefe

Unsinkable

I am your lifeboat
in the stormy waters
of our lives ...

in still waters
rocking you gently,
I lull you to sleep

hold you safe

You are my Anchor
holding me steady
I will never drift

away from you

sometimes we need to be anchored
and at others we need to set sail

together we can
keep our heads above water

Rhiannon Owens

Union

One man, one woman
Soul and body union,
Expressing their love
Well, they are only human,

Their wild imagination
So playful, so fun,
In secret intimacy
Coming together as one,

Now nine months later
Overjoyed and overcome,
An old life has ended
A new life's begun.

Ashley O'Keefe

A Betrayal of Souls

In silence, we stare
Eyes glimmer with tears,
Our crumbling world
In our furnace of fears,

Salty drops fall
On a trembling chin,
One who has cheated
One who's with sin.

Sniffling nose tears
We sigh and we wipe,
A warm summer day
Turns into cold winter's night,

Emotional torture
Excruciating pain,
A betrayal of souls
Hearts lost down the drain.

Ashley O'Keefe

Seasons of Love

Love in the Spring
Love in the fresh air
Love in the buds shyly showing themselves
Love in a new intimacy coyly shared

Love in the Summer
Love on a sandy beach
Love in our sandy sandwiches
Love in our sandy reach

Love in the Autumn
Love in the sharp cool breeze
Love in the swirling orange, yellow and red
Love as we kick through those fallen leaves

Love in the Winter
Love as we kiss under bare-branched trees
Love as we huddle under blankets together
Love is us toasty warm and naked while the window sills freeze

Rhiannon Owens

Cast in Iron

Souls forged in Iron
Rising against the Masters
With a flag of blood

(Inspired by the Merthyr Uprising against the greedy
Ironmasters, 1831. The people marched under the Red Flag for
the very first time).

Caws a Bara

All is silence in the Ironworks
the workers downed tools and stormed the town
they didn't just want bread
they wanted cheese with it too,
they were tired of the pain
their faces etched with frowns.

The Ironmasters feared for their selfish lives
troops had to be sent for
to stamp out this powerful uprising,
but although the people did not win this time
they tried and now know that they can.
A spark of resistance has been ignited
in their hearts and in their minds.

Rhiannon Owens
(Inspired by the people who rose up against the Ironmasters in Merthyr
Tydfil, 1831. They chanted 'Caws a bara' which translates as 'cheese with/and
bread' - they didn't want to merely exist, they wanted to LIVE).

© Rob Amos, 2018

Highly Strung

A gathering crowd
Out in the street,
Ironmasters within
Drink and eat,

Banners and flags
A protesting mob,
Can't afford food
Can't find a job,

Inside the Inn
Masters licking their lips,
Finish their dinner
More fat on their hips,

Soldiers in kilts
Arrive to the jeer,
Line up in two rows
People stand and leer,

The riot act is read
A fight breaks out,
Many are killed
It's all for nowt

A scapegoat is found
A town highly strung,
From Cardiff Gaol
A young man is hung.

Ashley O'Keefe
(Inspired by that fateful day outside The Castle Inn, Merthyr Tydfil, in 1831).

Martyr

People gather
Heads held low,
He marches to
The gallows pole,
Thunder roars
Lightning strikes,
The rain pours down
He sways ... deathlike…

Ashley O'Keefe
(Inspired by the hanging of Richard Lewis, better known as Dic Penderyn, who died proclaiming the injustice of his death and forgiving those who caused it).

Mademoiselle Nanette

In the opulent French Court of Louis
and his Marie-Antoinette
there was no courtesan more sought after
than the insatiable Mademoiselle Nanette.

Head held high, neckline low
instigator of les liaisons dangereuses
her appetit sexuel lauded in sonnet and song
any noble or marquis she could choose.

She had a hankering for titillation
flirtatiously fingering a curl in her hair
a coquettish ploy, biting her lower lip
flashing neck, breast and shoulders so bare.
Often she was struck with a strong urge to kiss,
the craving and hunger of a woman with Barsorexia
for the dandified fops of these decadent times
to dally with such a naughty madame,
there really was nothing sexier.

Yet Mademoiselle Nanette was no common whore
no naive ingenue nor destitute strumpet,
accomplished and witty, with means of her own
no man so foolhardy to view her as fluff or crumpet.

Certainly the courts at this time,
were famed for depravity, debauchery and excess
but it was the unbridled strength of her desires
that made her such a success.
She was renowned for enthusiasm
her wanton firkytoodling,
the way she could skillfully have a man panting,
there was artistry to her rampant canoodling.

95

To glimpse, caress and suck on her dugs
men would come from all over France
she entertained them with aplomb and vigour
and even led King Louis a merry old dance.

Rhiannon Owens
***(Inspired by the colourful bawdiness of Mary Robinson (1757-1800) as
portrayed in the play 'Bitches Ball' (Penny Dreadful Theatre Co.) and Emile
Zola's 'Nana' amongst many others)***

Casanova Jac

Sharp, witty and charming
Hair powdered, scented and curled,
A gambler and seducer
Married women and virgin girls unfurled,

The Count of Farussi
Or The 'Chevalier de Seingalt',
Fictitious names he'd call himself
In the company of Pope and Cardinal,

Famous for his affairs with women
A womaniser and a cad,
In England, he would be mistaken
As quite a 'Jack the Lad'.

Ashley O'Keefe

Flesh and Bone

Armour shining with the same divine light
that radiates from her saintly face,
she and the horse are as one
lean and strong, and ready
muscles rippling beneath smooth, young flesh
as they join the skirmish.

They are flesh and bone.

A cloak of red and gold streams from her shoulders.
The Angels are with them
wings of vermillion and flame.
She hears their voices.
She knows her purpose.

The child turns her cool eyes to the Heavens
as the fire licks at her skin,
eager to consume and ravage her virginal body.

The Angels gather above
silhouetted in the sunshine;
they have always been with her
and soon she'll always be with them.

She burns but is not burning.
Why would she?
She is a maiden with fire in her belly
and ice in her veins.

Born of the blazing sun
and she is ready to go home,
where she can fly in defiance
with magnificent wings of red and gold.

Rhiannon Owens
(Inspired by Jeanne d'Arc - "The Maid of Orleans")

Nom de Guerre (War Name)

The Scarlet Pimpernel
Our hero's nom de guerre,
During the Reign of Terror
Madame la Guillotine filled the air,

A chivalrous English gent
With a secret identity,
Helping to rescue French aristocrats
From execution, they would flee,

Leading a double life
Seen as a wealthy fop,
In reality a formidable swordsman
Sir Percy Blakeney was the top,

A quick-thinking escape artist
Not even Marguerite knew his job,
Entranced by this man's elusive exploits
She saves him from Chauvelin's mob.

Ashley O'Keefe

Nobody's Fool

Llew le Fol, respected by none
the King's own fool,
a fool to everyone.

A merry figure in yellow and red
an oversized hat decked with bells
jingling gaily on his head,
the toes of his shoes curl upward
for he is a clown
in service of the King,
to dispel his moods and frowns.

Gales of laughter follow his clumsy tomfoolery
and courtiers clutch their sides at his barbed repartee,
they watch his acrobatics in appreciation
astounded by his agility
as he somersaults, cartwheels, tumbles
and they clap and cheer
when he lets his tight-encased legs
get all tangled and jumbled.

Llew le Fol, telling stories of old
he juggles, performs magic tricks
and thrills with slapstick or satire,
and impressions so bold.
A troubadour of some renown too
hopping around with his flute,
then surprising all with a voice so rare
as he enchants all with a song
while he plucks at his lute 😜😜
Llew le Fol, fool to himself
with an ill-thought-out joke
at the King's expense
was put out to pasture,

and the King's displeasure saw
his replacement by
a jester
of short stature.

Embittered Llew plotted revenge
he was a great wit, had a silver tongue
and the King he had a much-beloved daughter,
as fair and bright-eyed
as she was young.

He wooed her under starlight
wooed her with poetry and song,
she knew that together they'd make sweet music
in her eyes, Llew could do no wrong.

Llew and Gwendoline made their escape
lit by moonlight on a white steed,
away from the confines of the court
together revelling in freedom
heeding not that they might be caught,
too happy to be bothered
by such worrisome thoughts.

The pair will never be captured
the King's men they will evade,
for they will search for a fool
in yellow and red,
not an ordinary man
and his sweet maid.

Nobody would want to believe
she'd been captured by the fool
still less,
captivated by a fool
spirited away,

but Llew had managed to avenge himself
he'd defied the King and his rule.

Riding over meadow
with his beautiful bride,
wild roses strewn through her hair.
Riding over the hillsides
his love for her had blossomed
and she was beyond compare.

He is no longer 'le Fol'
and she is a Princess no more,
just the lady Gwendoline
and her own beautiful Llew,
two lovers free to love
the way that only lovers do.

Llew le Fol, a jewel in the crown.
Now he's a fool of none.
Llew le Fol,
Nobody's Fool,
he has outfoxed everyone.

Rhiannon Owens

The Whistles Blow

Stillness... silence all around
An eerie place and time,
Across the water; unfamiliar soils
Beneath a sun that doesn't shine,

Looking out across the quagmire
Overseeing 'No man's land',
Just one more 'final push'
They await their last command,

The mist, the barbed wire fencing
The cold, the dark, the gloom,
Remembering family and loved ones
On the way to meet their doom,

Writing that final letter
The last song before they go,
A life too young to leave
Their brothers they'll follow,

The time has come
The whistles blow,
They raise their heads
From the trench, they go,

Bullets rapidly scudding by
Piercing flesh and bone,
Fighting in a foreign land
In a country miles from home,

Bodies wrapped in wire and blood
Brothers lying in their bed,
Young faces dying all around
For you and me they bled.

Ashley O'Keefe

Not A Footnote

*A friendship crafted
from words and prose, inspiring
this shared adventure*

A Man in the Strangest Town

Sleepy… Timeless…
A tranquil place,
Immortalised by a poet
In a shed, he would trace,

Looking out across the water
Of this estuary town,
"The strangest in Wales"
He fell in love, he wrote down,

In a boathouse, inspired
The words began to flow,
Where 'Under Milk Wood'
Would develop and grow,

Of an evening, he'd frequent
His favourite drinking den,
To sample the ale
And relax with the men,

Cradling his beer
Writing poems of the day,
On cigarette packets
Swept up and thrown away.

Ashley O'Keefe

Chrysalis

No gentle emergence from the chrysalis here
nothing natural about any of this,
no sleepy roll or astonished tumble to the ground
blearily blinking and lazily swiping sleep from our bemused eyes.

We were hastily bundled into the pupae stage
and now he drags us from the safety of our stasis,
when we want to stay numb and cocooned.
Too drugged to unfurl our fledgling wings,
if they'd had a chance to develop, he'd have clipped them anyway.

These plump, pretty caterpillars
forever green now, bright taffeta skirts stilled.
Chloroform lets us dream still
but our nostrils are assaulted by the stench of formaldehyde
we see the grotesque pallid shapes suspended in those jars
are neither caterpillar nor butterfly.

Stubby little partially formed nubs we have,
destined never to ripen or swell,
never to blossom into the rich, blooming fullness
of maturity.
Pinned in place, eyes open wide
but sightless...
some of us tried to fly, to soar
but a sharp stake through the sternum meant
that we were never destined
to be butterflies at all.

Rhiannon Owens

Insignificant

On the horizon
The earth's star rises,
Spreading like gold
In all its guises,

Monoliths of concrete
Soaring out of the ground,
Shadows colliding
With geometric surround,

Across the cityscape
A jumble of shapes,
The streets run in grids
With its many escapes,

Between chaotic buildings
A network of streets,
People are walking
Where the traffic meets,

High up on the rooftop
Above all the din,
Of busy people rushing
Their heads in a spin,

A man stands to gaze
Across the bustling Metropolis,
Taking in the scenery
Working through the hypothesis,

Unpacking his equipment
Taking his time,
Setting up; preparing
To aid him in his crime,

Under God's heaven
Feeling like the King,
At that moment, insignificant
In a world full of sin,

Relaxing with a Coffee
Taking in the sights,
Reading a book
Taking in the heights,

Time to get ready
The phone alarm goes off,
Into prone position
Time to finish off his quaff,

Raising the rifle
A steady hand lifts the gun,
The cavalcade approaches
His work is almost done,

Through telescopic lens
Spying through the sight,
The Mark soon appears
He won't put up a fight,

Taking aim, crosshairs lock
On his target soon to die,
Squeezing the trigger, SILENCE…
As the bullet goes scudding by,

Suddenly an eruption
A spurt of blood and bone,
Through the eyes of the hunter
The Hitman works alone.

Ashley O'Keefe

Traces

A woven tapestry, so elegant
Bright coloured threads interlaced,
A strand on its own is nothing
When interlocked a 'Screenplay' is traced

Each thread, an element of craft
To help readers emotionally feel,
To touch inner humanity deeply
And experience the meaningful deal

The message inside the story
Or in the flaw of the protagonist,
Comes from the emotional journey
The theme from which it exists,

A structured work of art
A powerful story skillfully told,
With brevity, clarity and passion
A film blue-print to behold.

Ashley O'Keefe

Snowdrop

Born far too early
the doctors didn't hold out much hope
as they prodded my soundless baby
frowned over their stethoscopes.
Premature and dependent
on various machines
not able to breathe by herself
a tinier baby never seen.
I spent the days by her side
but sometimes I just couldn't cope
pacing corridors like a restless feral
too numb
too dazed
too confused
to even dare hope.

I'd never been religious
but still I tried a prayer
yet even in my darkest hour
I couldn't believe any God was there.

The hospital had a window
looking out upon a courtyard
and I saw some snowdrops growing
though the ground was cold and hard.
The petals were so tiny
just like my little girl
so delicate and fragile
but still they had unfurled.

I returned to gaze upon the snowdrops
through the following bleak days
admired the strength of the hardy blooms
as in the January winds they swayed.
Innocent and pure

somehow they acted as a balm
when I thought I'd hit rock bottom,
their gentle serenity made me calm.

I don't know how it happened
and don't try to second guess
but my daughter grew stronger
got better
so perhaps I had been blessed?

… but when I look at my beautiful girl
I know she's stronger than she appears
my delicate little flower
I've shed many thankful tears.

I named her after the snowdrops
because they come too soon
yet in spite of this
just like those flowers
My Snowdrop managed to bloom.

Rhiannon Owens

DEDICATIONS

Rhiannon:

I dedicate this book to my lovely Mum (Rose) and equally lovely Dad (Glynne) ♥

Also to my beautiful, patient Nicholas who doesn't do fiction but reined me in when my poems were leaving the readers behind. Love you babe ♥

Thanks to the people who have taken the time to read my ramblings along the way ♥

Big thanks to Ashley for your continued support - you've been fantastic ♥

The Sea of Adventure
(For ASLEY)

I stand lost and Insignificant
head whirling at all of the silvered words
and elegant prose,
awash with uncertainty and self-doubt
an ego of eggshells to be traversed
on tippy toes.

I see you by the old Truck Shop
your words are forged in iron
'It's this way'...
I follow you past the inn
where the people are uprising
and a blood-dipped flag sways.

You tell me 'Hurry, come on!'
as we pass the rowdy saloon
the crash of tables overturning,

bottles smashing
and who's that?
That shadow that looms?...

It's One Man
and he stands at the saloon doors
taking it all in his stride,
his hand rests casually
beside his gun
those varmints have nowhere to hide.

I think he looks just like Clint Eastwood
but certainly not like John Wayne,
'cause I'd recognise his stiff-legged gait
like he's been rogered up the backside
and is now in immense pain!

'We'll miss the boat' you call to me
as plastic carousel horses bob up, down
and past,
and behind them canters a Horse With No Name
determined not to be last.

A Postman waves to us
as he whistles a cheery tune,
happy to be delivering the letter
that will unite two lovers soon.

I'm running beside you now
though I've got a stitch,
I reach down to a girl
the rope falling away
as I pull her from a ditch.

Letters of the alphabet
form a myriad of words
whirling through the air

and forming a vivid rainbow.
Dazzled, I dance across it,
upon its iridescent glow.

I dance without a care!
Sparkling, shimmering, vibrant.
Dancing the way I do
when I think no one else is there.

Over the rainbow…
but you keep on running.
I slide down giggling,
land in liquid gold
and I'm soon back behind you,
because you know just where to go!
Parts of it are already written,
others have yet to unfold.

We're on a boat,
the land falls back
further and further away;
the Horsemen of the Apocalypse
gave chase,
but we've left them behind...
they won't be catching us today!

We see brave Caratacus,
he stands with his family
and people
on the distant shore,
with Togodumnus he stands shoulder
to shoulder,
while the bodies of the last of
the invading Roman soldiers
litter the blood-soaked floor.

We're sailing across a Sea of Words

we're rewriting history!
With a bloke named Kevin,
who wears green tartan Pants
but why he wears them
is a Mystery!

On waves of pages and ink
carried on a current of thought,
sentences and paragraphs
toss and turn,
and create a tempest;
a storm ...

Will we capsize?
Our limbs smashed,
bodies torn?
Little boat veering
from its intended course.
Might we end up in Runcorn?

There are flowers growing out of the wooden decking,
with blooms, our boat is much festooned.
A lone Snowdrop resilient at the centre
of a bizarre collection of ugly shoes.
Figures are boxing in the shadows
somewhere Gerry and his Pacemakers croon,
the sky is divided in half
blue with a flamingly, flamboyant Sun
is Starboard,
Port, a black vista with the mysterious Moon.

A cat gallops along the deck
ridden by a small, Welsh mouse
with a Little Pig zipping around on a skateboard,
bottles of rum are lying empty
so I'm guessing we must be soused.

In the sky around us
Seagulls and Butterflies soar,
while there are real Crows in the Crow's Nest
staring down at a knife on the floor.
You carry a cutlass as a weapon
for Kevin in the Pants, it's a catapult …

I check the holster at my hip
my weapon is just a bloody corkscrew
unless an army of wine bottles lay siege,
I think I'm ill-prepared for this trip!
… but you just smile and shake your head at me
and conjure up more words,
and we paint with our imaginations
a dreamscape both beautiful and absurd.

Now a Seahorse With No Name keeps pace
and an inflatable flamingo floats up high,
beside a Kite Without Strings.
Higher still, a space shuttle shuttles on by,
stardust and moonbeams guide us
while meteors take our breath away,
and it's waterfalls, not just comets
that stream through this phenomenal sky.

We eat some Lemons from Sicily
and watch as the Titanic reaches dry land,
while Boys Who Never Grew Up
but are no longer Lost
are watched by two little girls
who stand at the stern,
together, hand in hand.

Faces in the rocks beguile us
as do beautiful Sirens
with their treacherous song.
I'm petrified but you say it's ok

and the ice cracks
as I start to feel strong.

Ghosts of Memories all around,
sometimes there's darkness
a Succubus and an Incubus sneer,
but with Hera to guide us on our voyage
a Goddess parting the waters,
no evil can ever come near.

It feels like we're in a Screenplay
but one that never ends,
an infinite, exciting adventure
with so many stories to be told.

We're safe because we weave
a tapestry of words,
and with you in the crew
my pen's poised - and I am finally bold!

Rhiannon Owens

DEDICATIONS

Ashley:

I dedicate this book to all my family, here and passed.

Thanks to my wonderful wife Helen for putting up with all the writing, especially the dictation when we're driving on long journeys. Love you, Molly and Erin, so much.

A big thank you to Rhiannon for all your support and proof-reading my Screenplay – you've been an inspiration.

Breaking the Ice
(For RHIANNO)

The frozen glass of winter
The incessant rain of spring,
The forbidden shadows of love in summer
In a sapphic sea of gin,

An autumnal girl who cries too much
Because of an offensive charm,
I am no man of ice you know
I sleep out on a farm,

And every day the cockerel crows
And the sun does shine,
Winter Solstice in the air
Amongst the sands of time,

There is no need to apologise
For teetering on the edge,
Like those strangers in the night
The incubus and succubus in your hedge.

Just remember every morning
Of every waking day,

That bloody postman's whistle
As he walks that certain way,

Like a Snowdrop in your garden
Like that delicate little flower,
You're stronger now than ever
So, for Nick's sake take that shower,

But seriously...

I've seen you change, I've seen you grow
Now you howl back at the moon,
No more do you fear
No more lonely paths anytime soon,

Sshht... Sshht... Sshht...

Like Torvill and Dean across the ice
We've pushed each other on,
In search of our Bolero
To find rhyme and rhythm in song,

You're no longer trapped beneath the ice
Now you're dancing free,
I came along in my Titanic boat
And crashed into Rhianno's sea.

Ashley O'Keefe

Images from Pixabay.com or authors own.
Special thank you to Rob Amos for the Merthyr Rising illustration.

Printed in Great Britain
by Amazon

42626861R00075